For my friend, Phoebe Gilman
F.W.

For Gabriel and Apple, with thanks to Dr. Hok
N.L.

First American edition published in 2003 by Carolrhoda Books, Inc.

Carolrhoda Books, Inc.
A division of Lerner Publishing Group
241 First Avenue North
Minneapolis, MN 55401 U.S.A.

Website address: www.lernerbooks.com

Library of Congress Cataloging-in-Publication Data

Wishinsky, Frieda.
Jennifer Jones won't leave me alone / by Frieda Wishinsky ; illustrated by Neal Layton.— 1st American ed.
p. cm.
Summary: A young boy is annoyed by the adoration of a girl in his class, but when she goes away, he misses her.
ISBN: 0-87614-921-2 (lib. bdg. : alk. paper)
[1. Friendship—Fiction. 2. Schools—Fiction. 3. Stories in rhyme.]
I. Layton, Neal, ill. II. Title.
PZ8.3.W754 Je 2003
[E]—dc21 2002008720

Printed and bound in Singapore
1 2 3 4 5 6 – OS – 08 07 06 05 04 03

Jennifer Jones Won't Leave Me Alone

Frieda Wishinsky
Neal Layton

Carolrhoda Books, Inc. / Minneapolis

Jennifer Jones won't leave me alone.
She sits by my side.
She **SHOUTS** in my ear.

She tells me she loves me.
She calls me her "dear."

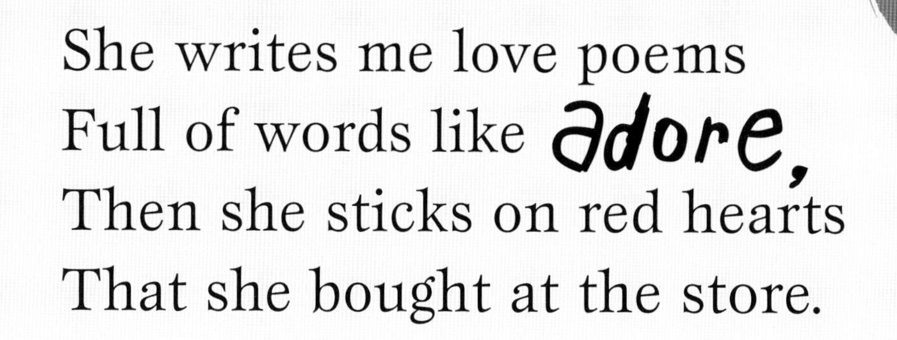

She writes me love poems
Full of words like adore,
Then she sticks on red hearts
That she bought at the store.

All my friends laugh and snicker.
They point and they stare.
They say,
YOU TWO MAKE SUCH A CUTE LITTLE PAIR!!
HAW!
TEE!

WELL, WE DON'T AND I HATE IT!

I've had quite enough.
I wish that she'd move
And take all her stuff.

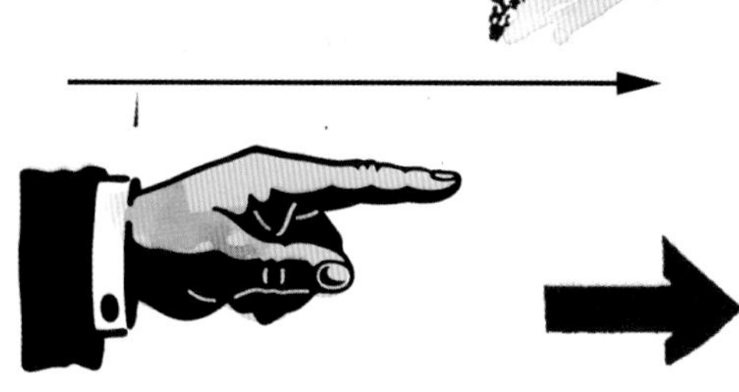

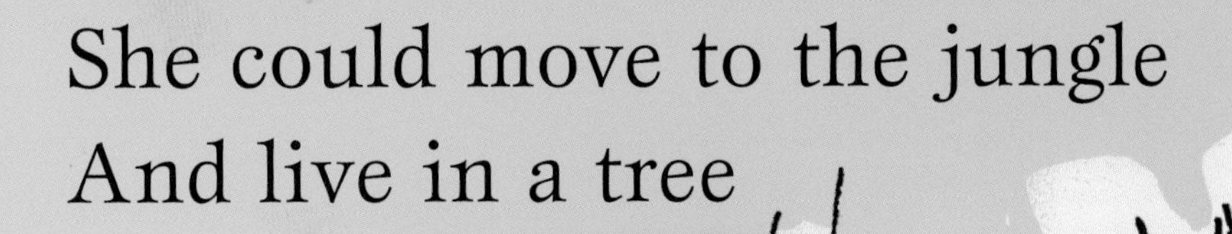

She could move to the jungle
And live in a tree

And talk to the monkeys,
Instead of to me.

But if she insists
That she's not going there,

She could head for the Arctic
And bother a bear.

I really don't care,
As long as it's soon.

Hip Hip Hooray!

Guess what I heard?
Jennifer's moving.
Her mom's been transferred.

“I’ll miss you,”
she said with a
tear in her eye.
Then she gave me
a kiss and whispered,

“Good-bye.”

Now her seat is all empty.
There's nobody there.
There's no one to kiss me.

There's no one to care.

So I write in my workbook.
I add and subtract.
I study my spelling.
I learn a new fact.

But it's boring! It's lonely!
I miss her a lot.
I wish she'd return

To her usual spot.

And to make matters worse
She writes, "It's divine
seeing paris at night,

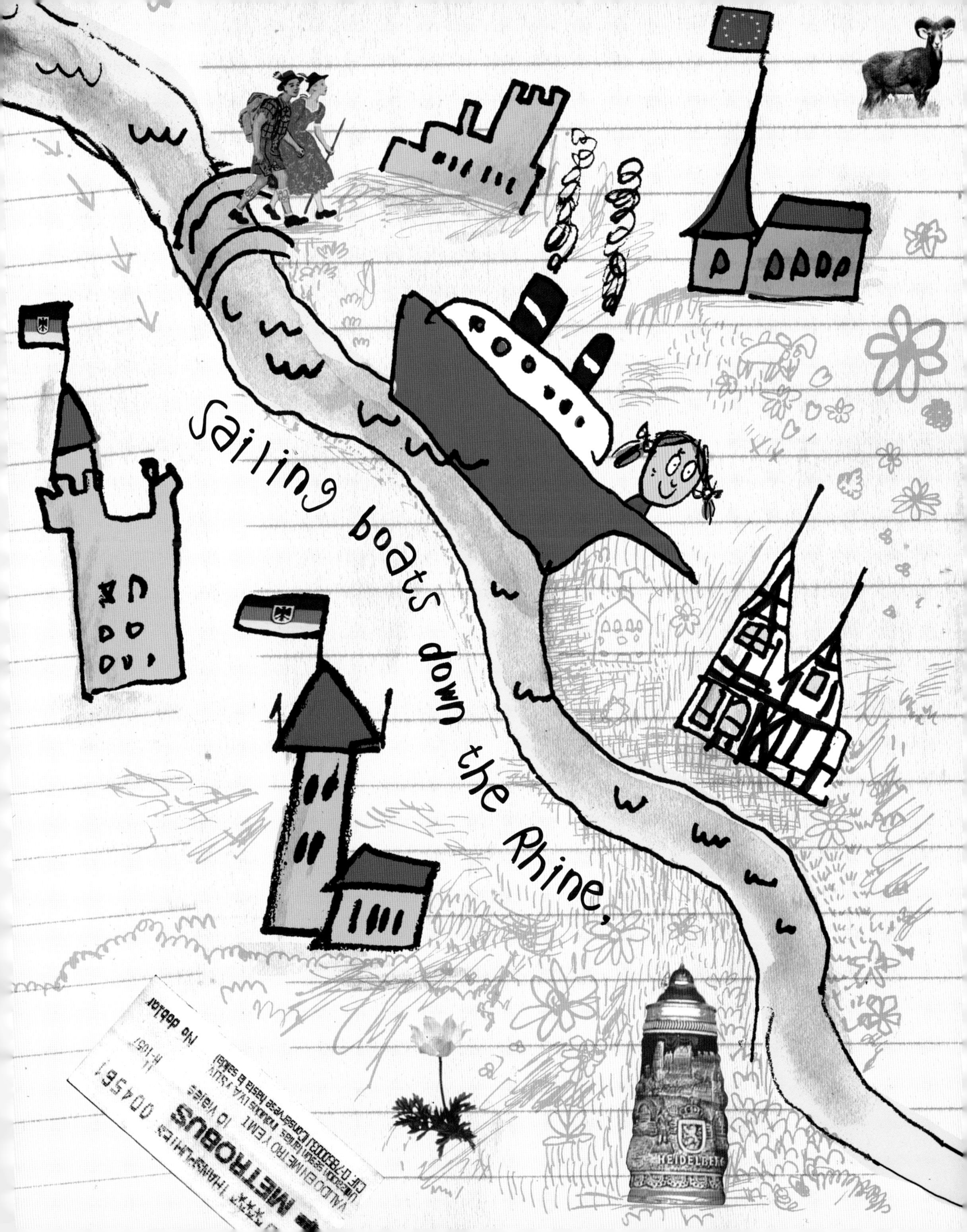
Sailing boats down the Rhine,
METROBUS
10 viajes
No doblar

Munching chocolates in Brussels,
CIAO!
Eating pizza in Rome,
CARTE POS
Cowley Rd
Oxford

Nibbling Viennese pastries you can't get at home."

Jennifer's having such fun,
I thought in despair.

She'll never come home.
She'll stay over there.

But then I read on,
"I'll see you in June."
And I yelled,

WHOOP-DEE-DOO!!!

She'll return very soon."

As soon as I did,
The kids asked me why
I was jumping and shouting.
So I thought,
should I lie?

But I told them the truth
As I opened the door.
Then I ran off to buy

Red hearts
at the store.

恋